NUGGET AND DOG

ALL KETCHUP, NO MUSTARD!

written and illustrated by
JASON THARP

Ready-to-Read *GRAPHICS*

SIMON SPOTLIGHT

An imprint of Simon & Schuster Children's Publishing Division • New York • London • Toronto • Sydney • New Delhi
1230 Avenue of the Americas, New York, New York 10020 • This Simon Spotlight edition June 2021
Text and illustrations copyright © 2021 by Jason Tharp • All rights reserved, including the right of reproduction in whole or in part in any form.
SIMON SPOTLIGHT, READY-TO-READ, and colophon are registered trademarks of Simon & Schuster, Inc. For information about special discounts for bulk purchases,
please contact Simon & Schuster Special Sales at 1-866-506-1949 or business@simonandschuster.com. Manufactured in the United States of America 0521 LAK
1 2 3 4 5 6 7 8 9 10 • This book has been cataloged with the Library of Congress.
ISBN 978-1-5344-8463-4 (hc) • ISBN 978-1-5344-8462-7 (pbk) • ISBN 978-1-5344-8464-1 (ebook)

To all the BIG dreamers,

Be yourself, stay kind, and try every day.
The right people will find you!
And to Beth, Laura, Siobhan, and Nicole,
K.E.T.C.H.U.P. Crusaders indeed!

—J. T.

Aunt Corny

Crouton
(say: KROO-tahn)

Dijon (say: dee-ZHON)
Mustard

Dog

Great-Grandpa
Frank Furter

Mayo Naze

Nugget

Tater Todd

Stomp

CONTENTS

How to Read This Book

This is Dog. He is here to give you some tips on how to read this book.

If there is a box like this one, read the words inside the box first. Then read the words in the speech or thought bubbles below it...

It's me, Dog! The pointy end of this **speech bubble** shows that I'm speaking.

When I'm thinking, you'll see a **bubbly cloud** with little clouds or circles pointing to me.

5

Chapter 1

FAST FORWARD TO NOW...

7

They are neighbors.

They are best friends.

They do everything together.

One day Great-Grandpa Frank Furter let them look for cool old stuff in his attic when...

Chapter 2

EVIL AND TANGY

DIJON

Chapter 3

Meanwhile, Nugget and Dog were opening the cool box.

That's it?!

A mask, a paper, and a photo?

We used K.E.T.C.H.U.P. to save Gastropolis.

Magic ketchup?

Ha, no. It was a different kind of ketchup. This ketchup was a way of life. Each letter of K.E.T.C.H.U.P. stood for something.

Kind
Empathetic
Thoughtful
Courageous
Helpful
Unique
Powerful

One day we found out that someone named Mayo Naze was making evil plans.

Through the power of K.E.T.C.H.U.P., we began to ruin Mayo Naze's plans by being so kind to her that she forgot to be mean.

Another time Mayo Naze was sick, and we brought her a get-well card.

It didn't happen right away, but over time the mold went away, Mayo Naze changed her ways, and Gastropolis returned to normal.

K.E.T.C.H.U.P. WINNER

MAYO

By the way, I think you know her great-grandson, Dijon.

What the **what!?**

It will have to do.

ZAP! ZAP!

UGHHH.

Stomp is alive!

Mwahaha!

Chapter 5

Meanwhile, Nugget and Dog were spreading K.E.T.C.H.U.P. all around.

EMPATHETIC

THOUGHTFUL

COURAGEOUS

39

40

43

45

Chapter 6

48

49

Chapter 7

Everyone thinks 'cause I'm small I can't do anything. I can do big things too.

Tater Todd, you just used **empathy**, a K.E.T.C.H.U.P. power!

Do you want to be my friends? Boy, I wish I had some beans to share.

Chapter 8

56

What are you doing, Stomp?! You're supposed to be an evil monster.

But Stomp is not bad. You are bad. You lied to Stomp!

You are not a good guy.

Chapter 9

They messed with the wrong mustard!

K.E.T.C.H.U.P. Crusaders might have won this time...

...but this is just the beginning of what Dijon Mustard can do. Mwahaha!

Mwahaha!